Step right up!
Come out of the rain!

Hop on board the Bunny Train!

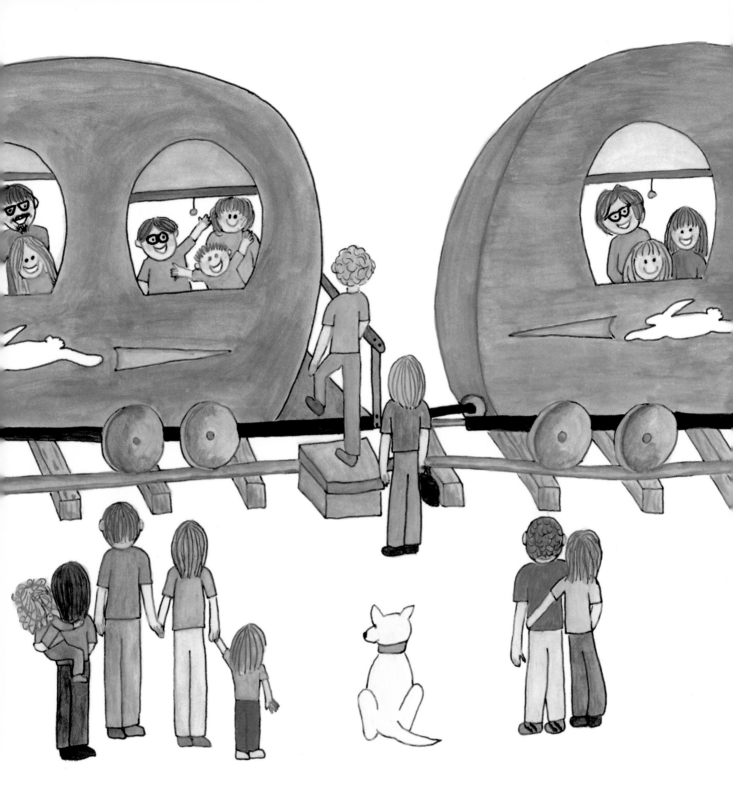

No need to shove, there's room for others.
Bring Mom and Dad, sisters, brothers.

3.

Please sit down. Better hold on tight!
She'll bounce and jounce to joy tonight.

The engine's cranked. Let's pause for prayer.
Her faith in God will chug us there.

5.

She pulls from the station. At last we depart.
All fired and fueled, she's got a full heart.

6.

She warms up fast. So happy we're here.
She waves us hugs with each floppy ear.

7.

Hippety-hop, Clickety-clack.
The cars are steady. She won't turn back.

8.

She whistles by farms. The cows
chew and moo. There's no time to stop.
Her paths are brand new.

9.

With Bunny Hopper hoots, she sings out her story
To send tales of hope delivered for God's glory.

10.

The music resounds from the front to the end.
Each car safely coupled around every bend.

The way sometimes hard. But she'll pass the test.
She doesn't slow down. She knows that she's blessed.

Her soul shines bright through tunnels dark.
She'll light our way. Don't disembark.

13.

Her steel is strong. She just keeps going.
Climbs over mountains. Her spirit showing.

14.

She'll lift us up to help us grow.
We'll gain great ground through fog and snow.

15.

If ticket sales are sometimes down,
it's hard to watch her wear a frown.

16.

he stops and thinks and asks, "What's wrong?"
"This railroad crossing seems so long."

17.

Her eyes look up, she knows what's wrong.
This railroad crossing won't take long.

18.

She sees the light change red to green.
God gives her go to sparkle and sheen.

The arms raise up. Her smile spreads wide.
Fasten your seatbelts for a rollercoaster ride.

20.

Transformed again she rears up high.
Look out world as she pilots to the sky!

Have you ever flown a train before?
No need to fear, our wings they soar.

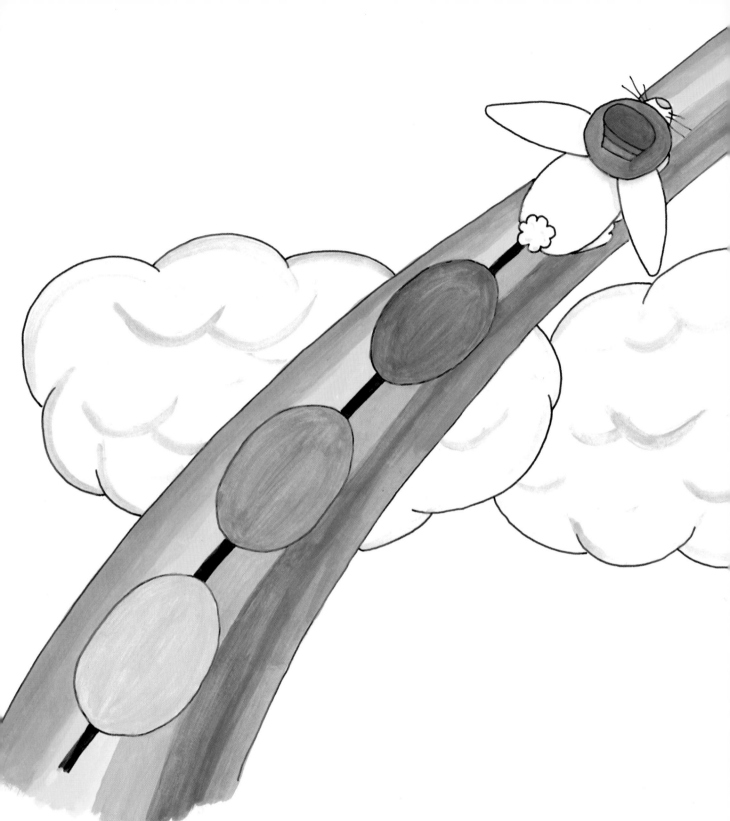

We'll clear storm clouds. Doubts fall to earth.
Reaching rainbows, we feel such mirth.

23.

We look below. The rail beds await.
We're oh so sleepy. It's now quite late.

24.

So-o-o jump back on The Bunny Train.
She'll take us home protected from the rain.
25.

God's her conductor guiding from above.
We'll pull through it all with Love, Love, Love!

26.

At last we're home all safe and snug.
When will we meet for us to hug?

27.

She seems such fun with all her hopping.
How does she do it without ears flopping?

28.

Please tell me now. Please tell me true.
Who is this train to me and you?

Now snuggle up. Come close and hear.
You'll recognize her by her cheer.

She's Mema, Granga, Grandma, Honey.
A friend to all. This story's Bunny!

The End.

32.